Little Princesses
The Cloud Princess

Little Princesses
The Cloud Princess

By Katie Chase

Illustrated by Leighton Noyes

Red Fox

Special thanks to Sue Mongredien

THE CLOUD PRINCESS
A RED FOX BOOK 9780099488392

First published in Great Britain by Red Fox,
an imprint of Random House Children's Books

This edition published 2007

3 5 7 9 10 8 6 4 2

Series created by Working Partners Ltd
Copyright © Working Partners Ltd, 2007
Illustrations copyright © Leighton Noyes, 2007
Cover illustration by Nila Aye

Set in 15/21pt Bembo Schoolbook

Red Fox Books are published by Random House Children's Books,
61–63 Uxbridge Road, London W5 5SA,
a division of The Random House Group Ltd

Addresses for Random House Group Ltd companies outside the UK
can be found at: www.randomhouse.co.uk

THE RANDOM HOUSE GROUP Limited Reg. No. 954009
www.**kids**at**randomhouse**.co.uk

The Random House Group Limited makes every effort to ensure that the
papers used in its books are made from trees that have been legally
sourced from well-managed and credibly certified forests. Our paper
procurement policy can be found at: www.randomhouse.co.uk/paper.htm.

Mixed Sources
Product group from well-managed
forests and other controlled sources
www.fsc.org Cert no. TT-COC-2139
© 1996 Forest Stewardship Council
FSC

A CIP catalogue record for this book is available from the British Library.

Printed and bound in Great Britain by
Cox & Wyman Ltd, Reading, Berkshire

For Abby and Becky French,
with lots of love – *S.M.*

For Mum and Dad,
with all my love and thanks – *L.N.*

Chapter One

"Thanks for the lift, Mrs Edwards," Rosie
Campbell said, getting out of the car. "Bye,
Emily."

"Bye, Rosie," Emily said from the back
seat.

"Goodbye, love," Emily's mum called. "And
remember to take off those muddy wellies
before you go indoors!"

Rosie nodded as Mrs Edwards drove away.
Rosie's boots were absolutely caked with
mud from her school trip to an archaeologi-
cal dig. The whole class had watched the
archaeologists use special tools to scrape
away mud from trenches as they hunted for

buried Roman artefacts. At the end of the day, everyone in Rosie's class had been allowed to have a go themselves, and Rosie had found a small orange tile! She'd been given special permission to bring it home to show her parents, before it went back to school tomorrow to be displayed with the other finds from the dig.

Rosie tramped up to the front door, carefully stepped out of her boots and went into the grand, echoing hallway. Although she'd been living in the castle for a while now, Rosie still found it hard to believe that this amazing place was actually her home. The castle belonged to Rosie's Great-aunt Rosamund, who was currently away travelling around the world. She had asked Rosie and her family to stay in the castle and look after it until she came back again.

Rosie hung up her coat, then went

through to the big, warm kitchen, where her
mum and her five-year-old brother, Luke,
were sitting at the table.

"Wall. W-A-L-L," Luke was saying as she walked in.

"Well done," Mrs Campbell said. She looked up at Rosie. "Hello, Rosie. Did you have a good day?"

"It was great," Rosie said. She held up her tile. "I found this on the dig. My teacher said that it could be a tile from a real Roman mosaic!"

Mrs Campbell came over for a closer look. Rosie handed her the little tile.

"I wonder where it came from," said Mrs Campbell, turning it over in her hand. "It's amazing to think that it might have been part of a Roman mosaic made over a thousand years ago, isn't it?"

Rosie nodded eagerly.

"What's a mosaic, Mum?" Luke asked, coming over to see the tile.

"It's a picture or pattern that's made up of thousands of tiny little tiles," Mrs Campbell explained. "The Romans used to have them on their floors and walls."

"Tile. T-I-L-E," Luke said proudly. He grinned at Rosie. "I've got a spelling test tomorrow," he explained. "And I've just *got* to beat Anna this time. She's this girl in my class and she always comes top at spelling. I can't keep getting beaten by a yucky girl!"

Rosie laughed. "Girls aren't yucky, Luke," she said.

Mrs Campbell passed Rosie's tile back to her. "You should have a look at the mosaic upstairs," she said. "It's on the wall of the northern passageway."

★ 5 ★

Rosie nodded. She'd seen the mosaic before but hadn't paid much attention to it. It was in a particularly draughty stone passageway, so she tended to rush past it as quickly as she could. "I'll go and look at it right now," she said enthusiastically, and headed off in the direction of the stairs.

One of the things she loved most about living in Great-aunt Rosamund's castle was the seemingly endless number of treasures that

there were to discover. Rosie's great-aunt had
ventured to almost every part of the world,
bringing back all sorts of unusual things.

But the thing Rosie loved more than
anything else was the fact that there were
little princesses hidden all around the castle!
Great-aunt Rosamund had left Rosie a
message telling her to look out for them.
At first Rosie hadn't understood, but then
she'd found a little princess in a picture
on her bedroom rug. Now, every time
Rosie saw a princess and said "hello" to
her, she found herself whisked away on an
extraordinary adventure!

Rosie was now in the northernmost side
of the castle, which got the least sun. She
shivered and pulled her school cardigan
more tightly around herself as she ran along
the passage. This is why I never come along
here, she thought. It's freezing!

Rosie turned a corner and spotted the mosaic on the wall a little way ahead. As she drew level with it, she stopped and gazed at it in fascination. It was enormous, longer than Rosie's arms spread out wide, and almost as high as she was. If you stood right up close to the mosaic, all you could see were the thousands of tiny individual ceramic tiles that made up the picture. But as you edged back, and looked at the mosaic as a whole, the picture took shape before your eyes.

The mosaic was edged with a twisty geometric border in red and brown. In the background of the picture itself stood a palatial villa that looked just like the Roman palace Rosie had been studying at school. It had white walls, a terracotta tiled roof, and five marble columns in the centre of the building.

In front of the palace, an old man lay

stretched out on a couch. Leaning over him, looking anxious, was a young girl in a white toga with a golden circlet around her head. Rosie felt her heart start to beat more quickly. She was sure that the girl was a little princess!

"Hello," Rosie said to the girl, making a neat curtsey.

All at once, a breeze streamed out of the mosaic, enveloping Rosie in the scent of lavender and the sweet taste of honey. The breeze became a whirlwind, and lifted Rosie right off her feet. Another adventure was beginning . . .

Chapter Two

The whirlwind slowed, and Rosie felt her feet
touch the ground again. She looked around
curiously. She was in a formal garden, with
neatly trimmed rectangular lawns, edged
with flowering lavender bushes. There was a
white marble building in front of her, with
stone columns at the entrance. Inside the
building, Rosie could see a girl kneeling
before a stone altar, with a large basket of
fruit and bread by her side. Rosie guessed
that the building must be a temple.

The girl was dressed in a white toga,
edged with a purple stripe. She had light-
brown hair, coiled up neatly in a knot on

top of her head, and she carried a satchel on one shoulder.

Rosie hastily looked down at herself and saw that her school uniform had disappeared. She was now wearing a white toga, with a red sash over one shoulder. The sash was pinned to the white material with a sparkly brooch of red stones set in gold. Around her arms were golden circlets that shone in the sun. Rosie reached up to touch her hair and found that it was coiled up neatly on top of her head.

I'm in ancient Rome, Rosie thought, feeling tingly with excitement.

Just then, the girl in the temple turned away from the altar and began to walk towards the entrance. Rosie saw that her shoulders were slumped and she looked very dejected. As she stepped outside, she noticed Rosie for the first time, and her mouth fell open with surprise.

Rosie smiled. "Hello," she said. "Are you a princess?"

The girl nodded. "I am Princess Isidora," she replied. Then she narrowed her eyes suspiciously. "Juventas? Is that you in disguise?"

Rosie shook her head, wondering who Juventas might be. "No, I'm Rosie," she said firmly. "I've come here by magic."

At Rosie's last words, the princess's eyes widened. "Magic?" she repeated in wonder. "Well, you must be a goddess then! You *are* Juventas!" she cried, throwing herself upon her knees.

"Please, I beg you," she went on. "*Please* remove the curse on my brother and the other boys in Rome. I will do anything you ask!"

Rosie blinked in surprise. "I'm sorry, but I'm really not Juventas, or any kind of goddess," she said, wondering what the princess was talking about. "I was only able to come here by magic because my great-aunt told me how."

"Oh!" Princess Isidora said, getting to her feet, and looking thoughtful. "My grandmother used to tell me stories about her friend, Rosamund, who used to visit by magic. But I always thought it was just a story."

Rosie smiled. "Rosamund is my great-aunt's name," she explained.

The princess's face lit up. "My grand-mother told me that Rosamund was a good

friend and helped her many times," she said.
"I think you have come at just the right
time, Rosie!"

"Why? What's wrong, Isidora?" Rosie
asked. "Can I help?"

The princess gave her a grateful smile.
"Call me Izzy," she told Rosie. "All my
friends do. And if you're offering to help, then
you're *definitely* a friend." She slipped an arm
through Rosie's, and they began walking
through the garden together.

"My brother Marcus turned sixteen two
days ago," Izzy began. "After his birthday
ceremony, when he received an adult toga
for the first time, he was supposed to leave a
coin on the temple altar as an offering to
Juventas."

"Who is Juventas?" Rosie asked.

"She is Goddess of Youth," Izzy explained.
"And on your sixteenth birthday, it is the

custom here to leave her an offering." She sighed heavily. "But Marcus, being Marcus, forgot about the offering, and went off to celebrate with his friends instead!"

At that point, the two girls came out into a sunny courtyard, and Rosie saw an elderly man sleeping on a couch in the sunshine. The man's face was lined with wrinkles, his hair was white, and Rosie could see that his hands were knotted and gnarled with age. She wondered if he was Izzy's grandfather.

"Juventas flew into a rage when Marcus forgot about the offering," Izzy went on, lowering her voice as they approached the old man. "She declared that if the emperor's son wouldn't show her respect, then she would show him her wrath. And so, as a punishment, she has made Marcus – and all the boys in Rome – age really quickly." Izzy pointed to the man on the couch. "See that man there?" she whispered.

Rosie nodded.

"That's Marcus," Izzy said. "He has gone from being sixteen to sixty in just two days!"

Chapter Three

Rosie stared in horror. She couldn't believe that the old man before her was really a sixteen-year-old boy! "What can we do?" she asked Izzy in a whisper. "Is there anything that will change Juventas's mind?"

Izzy shrugged helplessly. "Marcus and I have taken offerings to Juventas's temple every day, and prayed to her for hours," she said miserably. "But she is unmoved. The curse stands." Izzy gazed up at the sky, then turned to Rosie with tears in her eyes. "You know, Marcus and I used to play a game all the time," she said softly. "It was called the cloud game. We'd both lie on the grass, look

up at the clouds and try to see shapes in them — like a bird, or a face, or a tree. But now that Marcus has aged so much, he's too tired to play." She sighed again. "He keeps falling asleep in the middle of our game, or he complains that the light hurts his eyes. He has aged so quickly that in just a day or two more, he could die. And he won't be alone! All the other boys in Rome face exactly the same fate!"

"Isn't there anybody who could speak to Juventas for you?" Rosie said quickly. "Surely somebody can convince her that the boys have been punished enough?"

Izzy shook her head. "We can only make offerings to the gods, we cannot speak to them directly," she said. "I wish that we could, but—" Suddenly she broke off, looking excited. "Actually I *do* know someone who might be able to help," she said eagerly.

"He's not actually a god, but he knows the ways of the gods and he is very wise."

"Who is it?" Rosie asked.

"His name is Acis the Faun," Izzy replied. "He is a magical being who is half man and half goat, and he looks after the forest and everything in it." She led Rosie away from Marcus and across the lawn, her step quickening as she spoke. "He might be able to help, and if it wasn't for you I would probably never have thought of him! Thank you, Rosie."

"You're welcome, Izzy," Rosie laughed. "Shall we go and find the faun now?"

Izzy nodded. "I've heard that he's very shy," she said, "so he might not want to be found. But we'll do our very best."

Izzy led Rosie to the edge of the palace gardens and into some woodland. The two girls walked through the trees until they came to a small clearing, where Izzy gestured to Rosie to sit down with her on a large rock.

"If we wait here really quietly, he may come out to see us," Izzy whispered.

The two girls sat very still. Rosie could hear birds singing above her head. Then

she heard the sound of hooves, softly
padding over the forest floor. Rosie looked
around, trying to see where the noise was
coming from.

Suddenly she saw
a face peeping
out from
behind a tree.
It was a man's
face, but he
had two sharp
little horns on
his head and
pointed, furry ears.
Rosie nudged Izzy. "Is that Acis?" she hissed.

Izzy turned her head, but at that moment,
the creature vanished behind the tree trunk.

"Acis? Is that you?" Rosie called in a soft
voice. "Please don't go!"

"Acis, it's Princess Isidora," Izzy added.

"Please will you speak with us?"

There was a moment of silence, and then the faun's face reappeared. He looked as if he was considering the girls' request. Then he stepped out of the trees and trotted towards them. Although the top half of his body looked just like a man's, Rosie now saw that he had the hind legs and tail of a goat.

He came over to the girls. "Good day, Princess Isidora," he said. "And good day to your friend."

"Hello, I'm Rosie," Rosie said politely.

Acis ducked his head shyly, and turned back to the princess. "What is it you wish to speak to me about, Princess?"

"The goddess Juventas," Izzy began. "She has laid a curse upon my brother, and he—"

But Acis was already nodding. "I know what she has done," he told the girls. "I have heard all about it, because so many creatures

 25 ★

have been coming to hide in the forest these past two days."

"Are they hiding because they are scared of Juventas?" Rosie asked. She was starting to feel rather scared of the fierce-sounding goddess herself.

Acis shook his head. "It is not Juventas they are scared of," he said. "It is the Harpies."

"Harpies!" Izzy echoed in terror. "Where?"

"What are Harpies?" Rosie asked.

Izzy and Acis exchanged glances. "The Harpies are the servants of Pluto, God of the Underworld," Izzy explained with a shudder. "They have the heads of women and the bodies of vultures, and they are horribly cruel and vicious." She turned to Acis. "But why are they above ground? Why have they left the Underworld?" she asked.

"Pluto has sent them," Acis replied grimly.

"And I am afraid it is because he wants to make sure that Juventas's curse will never be broken!"

Chapter Four

There was a terrible silence as Izzy and
Rosie took in Acis's words.

"But *why*?" Rosie cried. "Why doesn't
Pluto want the curse to be broken?"

"The world of the living exists in a fine
balance with the Underworld," Acis
explained. "I'm afraid that, with all these
boys ageing early," he went on, looking
apologetically at Izzy, "there will be many
extra souls journeying to the Underworld
soon. That means more subjects for Pluto,
making him even more powerful."

Izzy's cheeks flushed. "Of course! If all
these poor boys die early," she cried, "Pluto

will become the most powerful of all the gods. No wonder he wants the curse to stand."

Rosie put an arm around her friend. "Can't the other gods do anything to stop

Juventas and Pluto?" she asked Acis. "Surely *they* don't want Pluto to have all the power?"

Acis smiled gently at her. "I'm afraid that the solution to this problem is not in the hands of the gods," he told her. "As a mortal created the problem, so a mortal must solve it. It is a law as old as time."

Rosie squeezed Izzy's hand and took a deep breath. "So it's down to us to sort things out," she said determinedly. "Acis, please will you help us?" she asked.

Acis shook his head. "I'm sorry," he said, "but there is nothing I can do. Juventas is a powerful goddess. I cannot make her change her mind." He paused thoughtfully. "However, there is one person who might be able to help you," he went on. "Cupid, God of Love. If you two can find Cupid, and persuade him to shoot Juventas with one of his special arrows of love, then you might

succeed in softening the goddess's heart and convince her to cancel the curse."

Izzy nodded. "That's a great idea," she said, sounding a little more cheerful. "Thank you, Acis. Where should we look for Cupid?"

"You will find Cupid wherever there is love," Acis replied. "And particularly where love is being celebrated." The faun knelt down and plucked a tiny white flower from the ground. "Take this," he said, passing it

to Izzy. "It is a magical flower. If you brush the petals across your eyes, you will be able to see Cupid and any other gods usually invisible to mortals."

"Thank you, Acis," Rosie said, as Izzy put the flower carefully in her satchel. "You've been very kind."

Acis bowed his head. "My pleasure," he said. "Good luck on your quest, but watch out for the Harpies. If they find out what you are trying to do, they will drag you off to the Underworld, and Pluto will have your souls!" And, with that, Acis disappeared into the forest.

The girls exchanged an anxious glance and headed back towards the palace.

"Where could Cupid be? I wonder," Rosie said thoughtfully. "Acis said that—" But she had no time to finish her sentence, for a terrible screech came from the sky, and Izzy

dragged Rosie down behind a pile of rocks.
"Quiet, Rosie!" Izzy hissed fearfully. "That
was the cry of a Harpy!"

Chapter Five

Rosie shrank against the rocks, her heart thudding. She could hear the sound of beating wings, and then another blood-chilling screech echoed over the forest. The foul, choking stench of decay filled the air. Cautiously Rosie tipped her head back so that she could peep upwards. There, just above the treetops, hovered a large dark shape.

The creature had ragged, black wings, and the body of a great bird. But its head and face were those of an old woman. Tangled hair blew around its face, and the Harpy suddenly let out another horrible screech so

that Rosie
glimpsed two rows of rotten,
yellow teeth in its mouth.

The Harpy circled above the treetops,
shrieked once more, and then headed off
away from the forest. Rosie felt herself relax
slightly as the Harpy disappeared from view
and the smell faded. "That was really scary,"
she said. "Let's get out of here, fast!"

Izzy nodded wholeheartedly. "Definitely," she said. "We need to find Cupid right away. Where could he be?"

"We'll find him somewhere where love is celebrated," Rosie said, remembering Acis's words.

"In the Temple of Venus?" Izzy wondered.

"Or maybe at a wedding?" Rosie suggested.

Izzy's face lit up. "Good thinking!" she said. "I know where a wedding is taking place this very afternoon – one of my father's advisers is getting married!" She grinned at Rosie. "We'll go to his villa. Cupid will surely be somewhere there."

Izzy led Rosie out of the grounds of the palace and onto a long, straight road. The girls kept checking the sky for any sign of Harpies, but, thankfully, there was no sign of the terrible creatures. Rosie began to take in the scenery around her.

They passed one man who was sitting outside his home, carefully shaping a clay bowl on a stone slab. Further along was a bakery, with trays of fragrant fresh bread piled up outside. Then they reached a well, where women filled large clay pots with water for their families.

After a while, Izzy pointed to a villa which was set back from the road. "This is it," she said, stopping. "And listen! Can you hear the music? Here comes the wedding procession!"

Rosie turned her head towards the faint sound of approaching music. In the distance, she saw a great crowd coming towards her, and some of the people were playing drums and pipes. She and Izzy watched as the procession passed them and entered the courtyard of the villa. At the rear of the procession was a woman wearing a flame-coloured veil. She was surrounded by female

attendants who each carried a flaming torch.

"That's the bride," Izzy whispered to Rosie. "And any minute now, the wedding feast will begin. Follow me."

Rosie followed Izzy as the princess fell in with the wedding procession. Soon she found herself in the villa's large courtyard with the other wedding guests. As everybody watched, the bride was handed a flaming torch by one of her attendants. She lifted her veil and blew out the flames in one strong breath. Everybody cheered, and the bride waved the smoking torch in the air and then threw it into the crowd. The guests scrambled to catch it, and Rosie smiled. It was just the way she'd seen brides throw their flower bouquets at weddings she'd been to with her mum and dad. A dark-haired woman with a large silver necklace caught the torch and held it up triumphantly. The crowd roared in approval, then drew back as servants began bringing out trays of food and drink. Rosie saw lots of meat – including a whole suckling pig on a platter – and bowls of bread, olives, cheese, fruit and nuts.

"Let's see if we can spot Cupid anywhere," Izzy whispered to Rosie.

Rosie nodded. "Let's use the magic flower from Acis," she suggested.

Izzy nodded, opened her satchel and took out the magic flower. She brushed it carefully across her eyes, and then gave it to Rosie.

Rosie brushed the flower over her eyes too, and felt a warm sensation spread across her eyelids. Then the girls made their way among

the wedding guests, who were now singing a celebratory wedding song.

As Rosie walked through the crowd, a flicker of movement in the air caught her eye. She turned to look quickly, fearing another Harpy was approaching, but what she actually saw was a small, winged boy, hovering in mid-air! He was about the same age as Luke, she guessed, and he wore a golden toga, with a bow and a quiver of arrows slung over his shoulder.

"Izzy, is that him?" Rosie hissed to her friend, pointing towards the boy.

Izzy grinned. "It certainly is," she said. "Let's see if we can get him to come down and talk to us."

The girls crossed the courtyard to the place where Cupid was floating.

"Excuse me, could you come down here for a moment please?" Rosie asked politely.

Cupid jumped at the sound of Rosie's voice, and stared down at her with an expression of horror and amazement on his face. Then he looked all around, as if he thought Rosie might be talking to someone else.

"Cupid!" Izzy said, a little louder. "Will you come here, please? We need to speak to you."

Cupid stared at her as if he could hardly believe his eyes. "Are you talking to me?" he asked hesitantly.

Izzy nodded. "Yes," she said. "You're Cupid, aren't you?"

"Yes, I am, but . . ." Cupid clutched his bow and arrow rather defensively. "Can you actually *see* me?"

"Yes," Rosie said, frowning, "we can, so will you—?"

But before she could finish her question, Cupid zipped behind a stone pillar so that only the tips of his wings were visible. "*Now* can you see me?" he demanded.

"Yes!" Izzy said, rather impatiently. "We can still see you."

Cupid flew swiftly to the banqueting tables and hid behind the suckling pig. This time the girls could still see his bow and arrows. "What about now? Can you see me now?" he said.

Rosie and Izzy exchanged puzzled glances. "Yes," Rosie told him.

"So will you *please* stop messing about and come and talk to us?" Izzy cried. "We need your help!"

Cupid flew over to them. "But how can you see me? How?" he demanded. "Mortals are only allowed to see me when I give them permission. And there's no way I'd ever let a pair of yucky girls see me!"

Rosie told Cupid about the flower that Acis had given them. "And Acis thought you might be able to help us soften Juventas's heart," she said, "so, will you?"

"He thought you might use one of your special arrows, you see," Izzy explained.

Cupid snorted indignantly. "Well, Acis thought *wrong*," he retorted, folding his arms, "because I'm not helping pesky girls with anything. You might as well go away, right now!"

Chapter Six

There was a moment of silence as the two girls watched Cupid fly away from them. Then they exchanged a look of alarm, and ran after the grumpy god.

"I thought you were meant to be God of Love!" Rosie burst out indignantly as they caught up with Cupid. "Why do you hate girls? Surely you should love everyone?"

Cupid sniffed disdainfully. "The God of Love stuff is just a job," he said, "and it isn't even fun! All the other gods laugh at me!" He stuck out his lower lip sulkily, reminding Rosie of her little brother, Luke.

"And as if that's not bad enough," Cupid

went on, "all my friends in the mortal world have suddenly grown really old! See those two?" He pointed his bow in the direction of two old men, who were hobbling along on sticks. "They were young boys a few days ago," Cupid said, "and they were really fun friends of mine. But now they're old men and they're no fun *at all*!"

As Rosie watched the elderly men, she noticed that several of the guests were staring quizzically at her and Izzy. Rosie wondered why, until she remembered that none of the other guests could see Cupid and realized that it must seem to them as if she and Izzy were talking to thin air!

Quickly she reached up, grabbed Cupid's hand and dragged him over to a quiet corner, where they would all be hidden by a large flowering shrub. "People are looking at us," she murmured to Izzy, who had followed her.

"Get off! Ugh!" moaned Cupid, trying to wrestle his hand out of Rosie's. As soon as Rosie let go, he shot backwards, cleaning his fingers fussily on one of his wings, as if she had contaminated him in some way. "YUCK!" Cupid muttered, glaring at her. "Holding hands is for *girls*. I don't want any girl-ness rubbing off on *me*!"

Rosie exchanged a smile with Izzy. *Honestly!* she thought. Not even Luke would make such a fuss about a bit of hand-holding! As she thought of her brother, an idea popped into Rosie's head. After all, Luke wasn't particularly keen on girls either.

Maybe she could use Cupid's feelings to her advantage . . .

Rosie heaved a theatrical sigh. "Oh, it's a shame you don't like girls," she said, trying to sound as woeful as possible. "Because if Juventas isn't stopped soon, you will only have girls left to play with . . ."

Izzy caught Rosie's eye and grinned. She had obviously guessed exactly what Rosie was plotting.

Izzy looked up at Cupid sympathetically. "Don't worry," she said, in a soothing voice, "you won't be lonely; I'll bring some of my friends over for you to meet. You'll have a lovely time with them, playing tea parties with dolls, and dressing up, and . . ."

Cupid turned pale. "That sounds *awful*," he said, with feeling. "But what can I do? I can't shoot Juventas! She's one of the most powerful goddesses in the heavens! My mum would *really* tell me off if I got into trouble with Juventas!"

Rosie shrugged. "Oh, well," she said, turning away as if she was about to leave. "Never mind."

"Looks like we'd better count you in for those tea parties then," Izzy added.

"All right, all right," Cupid said quickly. "I'll give you an arrow to soften up Juventas, but I'm not shooting her for you." He rummaged in the quiver that held his arrows and pulled out a long, slender, gold-tipped bolt.

"This will melt the hardest heart as soon as it touches the skin," he said proudly, passing it over to Izzy. "That's the best I can do. Will you leave me alone now?"

"Thank you, Cupid," Izzy said, tucking the arrow carefully in her satchel. "And of course we'll leave you alone — just as soon as you tell us how we can reach the Garden of Heaven where the gods live."

"You'll have to fly there, of course," Cupid said, and then he gave an enormous sigh. "Except you can't fly, can you?" he said,

shaking his head at the girls' ineptitude.
"And before you ask, no, I won't carry you
there on my back." He gazed around the
courtyard as if looking for inspiration. Then
his eyes fell upon a bench, where a young
man lay sleeping. "See him over there?
Sleepyhead? That's my Uncle Mercury.
He's God of Travel," Cupid told the girls.

Rosie saw that the god was stretched out
asleep with his feet dangling over the end
of the bench, and on his feet were leather
sandals with tiny white wings at the heels.

"If you really want to fly to the Garden of Heaven," Cupid said, "you're going to have to borrow Mercury's shoes."

Izzy looked doubtful. "Won't he mind?" she asked.

Cupid stared scornfully at her. "We're not going to *ask* him!" he explained. "You just bring the sandals back before he wakes up, and he never has to know you borrowed them."

Rosie bit her lip, feeling uncomfortable with the thought of borrowing the sandals without Mercury's permission. "I don't know if this is a good idea," she said.

Izzy sighed. "Neither do I," she agreed, "but we've come this far, and we've got to try to get to the Garden of Heaven, for the sake of all the boys in Rome!" She gazed at the winged sandals. "We'll just have to go quickly, and get the shoes back to

Mercury as soon as we can!"

Rosie nodded. "So, how do we get the shoes off his feet?" she asked. "Is there a magical way you can do it, Cupid?" she added hopefully.

Cupid laughed. "Nope!" he replied. "You two will have to take them off yourselves." He grinned cheekily. "Only, don't wake him up, will you? My Uncle Mercury has a *ferocious* temper!"

Chapter Seven

Rosie gulped. Not another bad-tempered god! She looked at Izzy, who was looking at the sandals determinedly.

"We'll just have to be very careful," the princess said.

Rosie nodded. "Come on, then," she murmured, trying to sound confident. "Let's do it while he's still fast asleep."

The two girls went over to Mercury and crouched down by his feet. The god's sandals were made out of brown leather and had thick ties around the ankles. They looked quite ordinary – until you saw the most *extraordinary* pair of white feathery wings that sprouted from the heels.

Rosie pointed at Mercury's left sandal, and Izzy nodded. Rosie edged closer to Mercury's foot and took a very gentle hold of the knotted ankle tie. Very carefully she unfastened the leather tie, and Izzy swiftly

unwound the lacings and eased the sandal off Mercury's foot.

Then the girls both took a deep breath and moved over to Mercury's right foot. Just then, Mercury's eyelids twitched, and he muttered something in his sleep. Rosie and Izzy froze, staring at each other in fright. Seconds passed, and then a deep throaty snore came from the sleeping god.

Rosie quickly untied the leather string that wound around Mercury's right ankle and, again, Izzy eased off the sandal. They had done it!

Rosie grinned as they retreated behind the flowering bush once more and showed Cupid the sandals.

"I think you'll be all right with one each," Cupid said, eyeing the sandals appraisingly. "You're much smaller than Uncle Mercury. But I think you'll have to hold hands to keep

your balance. The sandals are used to
working as a pair, after all."

Rosie felt her heart thumping with excitement as she kicked off her shoes and tied one
of Mercury's sandals onto her left foot. She
could hardly believe she was about to fly!

"So, how do they work?" Izzy asked
Cupid as she firmly attached the other
winged sandal to her right foot.

"To take off," Cupid instructed, "you each have to stamp your winged foot once, and imagine yourselves to be as light as possible. The lighter you can imagine yourselves, the faster you'll fly."

Rosie and Izzy smiled at each other and held hands.

"Think light!" Cupid urged them.

"Feathers!" Rosie said aloud.

"Butterflies!" Izzy called out.

"A rose petal!" Rosie laughed.

"Each stamp your winged foot . . . now!" Cupid urged.

Rosie and Izzy did as Cupid instructed, and suddenly they were shooting above the wedding party, up into the sky.

"Wow!" Rosie exclaimed breathlessly. "We're flying, Izzy! We're flying!"

"Whoa!" Izzy yelled, as Rosie soared higher than she did. "We're going to tip up!"

"Keep thinking light things!" Cupid cried, hovering alongside them. "You're uneven; you need to balance yourselves!"

"Um . . . the fluff from dandelion clocks!" Izzy called out. Immediately she surged higher, but now she was higher than Rosie.

Rosie felt her arm being pulled to stretching point. "Thistledown!

I'm as light as thistle-down!" she yelled, and up she rose. Now Rosie was the highest and, because the two girls were so lop-sided, they began to flounder and cartwheel in the air.

"Well, we won't get very far like this," Rosie giggled. "Let's think of the same thing

this time. Let's *both* imagine that we're as
light as thistledown."

"OK," Izzy agreed.
"I'm as light as
thistledown. I'm as
light as thistledown,"
she told herself.

She bobbed up to the same
height as Rosie then, and the girls grinned at
one another.

"It looks like we've got the hang of flying
now," Rosie said. "We should get going."

Izzy nodded. "Wait, Cupid's coming," she
said, pointing to the god, who was zooming
up towards them.

"I wonder what he wants," Rosie said,
puzzled. "I thought he couldn't wait to see
the back of us."

The girls watched as Cupid approached.
"You have to go now!" he called frantically.

"Go to the Garden of Heaven at once. There are Harpies on the horizon! And Harpies are even worse than *girls*!" He pointed off into the distance.

Rosie turned her head to look where Cupid indicated, and saw three dark figures approaching rapidly.

"I'll distract them for as long as I can," Cupid shouted. "I'll shoot my arrows at them. There's no way they'll want to be hit by one of those; Harpies are seriously allergic to love!"

"Thanks," Rosie gulped. "Come on, Izzy, let's go."

Izzy nodded, looking pale. "Think thistledown again," she said. "We are as light as thistledown!"

The girls flew off quickly, climbing higher and higher in the sky, until Cupid was left far behind.

"Phew," Izzy panted in relief, as they neared a layer of cloud. "I'm glad we managed to escape the Harpies."

Rosie was just about to agree when she glanced back down and saw the dark shapes of the Harpies closing on them. "Izzy, we haven't escaped yet!" she gasped in dismay. "The Harpies are catching up! We need to go faster."

"What other light things can we think of?" Izzy cried out urgently. "My mind's gone blank!"

"A . . . snowflake!" Rosie shouted. "We're as light as snowflakes!" They surged upwards, higher and faster, but still the harpies drew closer.

"A cat's whisker!" Izzy exclaimed, but the Harpies continued to gain on them.

"Smoke!" Rosie panted. She could hear the flap of the Harpies' ragged wings now, and smell the choking stench of decay floating up through the air.

"Rosie, look out!" Izzy screamed. "There's a Harpy right behind you!"

Rosie glanced over her shoulder and saw the hideous face of a Harpy only inches away from her own. Its mouth was stretched into an evil grin, and its foul stench caught in Rosie's nose and throat. As she coughed and choked, the creature reached towards her with vicious talons.

Chapter Eight

Rosie instinctively drew her legs up away from the Harpy, and the creature's claws slashed through the air inches from Rosie's right ankle. Rosie knew that she and Izzy had to think of something *really* light now, if they were to get away and reach the Garden of Heaven.

Then Rosie realized that the answer was all around her – clouds. "We're as light as clouds!" she bellowed at the top of her lungs. "White, fluffy clouds."

"Yes! As light as clouds!" Izzy echoed desperately.

Immediately the girls found themselves

shooting upwards at a fantastic rate. The
Harpies screeched in fury as the girls pulled
away from them and burst through the wispy
white layer of clouds.

As they emerged above the cloud layer,
Rosie caught sight of some huge golden
gates ahead, standing ajar. "Look!" she
shouted to Izzy.

"The gates to the Garden of Heaven!" Izzy
cheered. "Quick, we're nearly there!"

The girls zoomed towards the gates, swerved inside and slammed the gates behind them with a loud clang.

The Harpies screeched in fury and rattled the bars with their talons, but the gates remained tightly shut.

Rosie and Izzy hugged each other in relief. "We made it," Rosie panted. "We're here in the Garden of Heaven at last."

"That was a stroke of genius to think of clouds," Izzy said warmly. Then she sniffed the air wonderingly. "How odd, I can't smell the Harpies any more. The gate must be keeping out nasty smells as well as nasty creatures!" She smiled. "Now, I wonder where we go to find Juventas . . ."

Rosie looked around and saw a tall man coming towards them. "I don't know, but somebody's just found *us*," she told Izzy in a low voice.

The man had seen the Harpies, who were
still rattling the gates. As he walked over to
address them, Rosie saw that the man had
two faces — one on the front of his head,
and another on the back!

"Creatures from the Underworld need
permission from Jupiter, Chief of the Gods,
to come to the Garden of Heaven," the man
said to the Harpies with a disapproving
frown. "Do you have permission from
Jupiter?"

The Harpies snarled and gnashed their teeth at him, and the tall man shook his head. "I didn't think so," he said, and turned back towards Rosie and Izzy.

"Good day," he said politely. "I am Janus, God of Doors. I am in charge of comings and goings – which is why I have two faces."

"Hello," Rosie said. "I'm Rosie."

Izzy smiled. "And I am Princess Isidora of Rome," she said, dropping a graceful curtsey to the god.

"Very nice to meet you," Janus said, smiling. "But I'm afraid I can't let you into the Garden of Heaven unless you have permission. *Do* you have permission?"

The girls shook their heads dismally.

"Well, are either of you minor gods?" Janus enquired.

"Um . . . no," Rosie admitted.

"Then perhaps you are the children of gods?" Janus asked hopefully.

"No," Izzy said. "But my father is Emperor of Rome and—"

"Then I'm afraid you will have to leave," Janus said, with an apologetic smile.

A horrible cackling came from the gates, and Rosie turned, with sinking spirits, to see that the Harpies were laughing nastily.

"Please let us stay," Rosie begged Janus. "We have to find Juventas and the Harpies will catch us if you throw us out."

Janus looked over at the Harpies and then back at the girls. He leaned towards them in a conspiratorial manner. "You know, I'm not a big fan of Harpies," he whispered, "and I *was* impressed by the way you out-flew them," he went on. "Perhaps if you can prove that you are intelligent as well as swift, I will let you in."

At his words, two golden doors materialized behind him. Both looked exactly the same, and both were tightly shut.

"One of these doors opens to the future," Janus said. "The other door opens to the past. I want you to tell me which door you think will lead to the Garden of Heaven."

Rosie looked at her friend. She really didn't know enough about the gods of Rome to guess herself. "What do you think, Izzy?" she murmured.

"Well, the gods are immortal, so they can

never die," Izzy said, pursing her lips thoughtfully. "Therefore the Garden of Heaven could be behind the *future* door." She paused for a second, thinking hard. "Then again, they have been around for centuries, so the Garden of Heaven could easily be in the past too." The girls shared an agonized look, wondering which door they should choose.

The Harpies were still cackling hopefully in the background and Rosie shivered. "We've got to get this right," she said urgently. "Otherwise the Harpies will carry us off to the Underworld!"

Chapter Nine

Rosie racked her brains, and then a thought struck her.

She turned excitedly to Izzy. "If the gods are immortal," Rosie began carefully, "that means they live for ever. And if they live for ever that means they are in the past *and* in the future. So maybe that's the answer: the Garden of Heaven lies behind *both* doors!"

Izzy nodded eagerly. "I think you might be right," she said, staring at the doors. "Janus didn't say we had to pick one single door, so let's pick them both!" She turned to Janus, and took a deep breath. "Janus, we think that both the door to the future *and* the door to the past lead to the Garden of Heaven," she said, watching him closely.

To Rosie's great relief, Janus smiled. "Well worked out," he said. "You are right. You have my permission to enter the Garden of Heaven."

The Harpies wailed and moaned as Rosie and Izzy grinned and hugged each other.

"Thank you, Janus," Izzy said, beaming. "Now, do you know where we might find Juventas?"

"Oh, just follow the sound of shouting," Janus told her. "Juventas has been in a terrible rage for days."

"Thank you," Rosie said, rather apprehensively.

The golden doors vanished to become a golden archway, and the girls stepped through to find themselves in a beautiful garden. There were bright flowers everywhere, and trees laden with oranges and lemons. Peacocks strutted through the grass, and iridescent butterflies fluttered from flower to flower. In the distance, a waterfall cascaded down a tumble of rocks and tiny rainbow-coloured birds darted low over the water.

"I can't hear any shouting," Izzy commented.

"Neither can I," Rosie said. "Do you think she's finally calmed down?"

Izzy shook her head. "I doubt it," she sighed. "Come on, let's look around."

The girls started to search the garden, but it was sunny and hot and soon they both needed a rest. They stopped by an ornate stone fountain, and Izzy put her satchel down while she went to take a drink.

Suddenly Rosie heard a low rumbling sound. "What do you think that is?" she asked curiously.

Izzy stood up and listened. The rumbling seemed to be getting louder. Now it sounded like an angry bellowing. "It's Juventas," Izzy said, wiping her mouth hastily. "Look, here she comes!"

Advancing along the path that led to the

fountain was a tall, dark-
haired woman ranting
crossly to herself.
Rosie couldn't help
thinking that if the
goddess would only
smile, she would be
really beautiful, but
right now, her features
were spoiled by her
angry frown.

The goddess stopped before the girls. "Who
are you?" she demanded suspiciously.

"Good day, great goddess," Izzy said,
curtseying respectfully. "I am Princess Isidora
of Rome, the sister of Marcus, the boy who
forgot to—"

"Silence!" Juventas thundered. "Don't you
dare speak of that boy! I never want to hear
his name again!"

"But I came to beg for your forgiveness—"
Izzy began.

But Juventas hadn't finished. "That boy has made me the laughing stock of all the gods!" she railed, and launched into a furious tirade about disrespectful youths.

While Juventas was shouting, Rosie took the opportunity to edge closer to Izzy's satchel. Quietly she reached down and felt inside for Cupid's arrow. Her fingers soon  closed around the arrow's stem and Rosie carefully withdrew it from the bag.

"He's terribly sorry for his mistake—" Izzy was saying soothingly.

"Good! So he should be!" Juventas snapped. "The other gods said that I'd lost my power over mortals!" she exclaimed in outrage. "Well, they can all see how powerful I am, now that the boys of Rome have withered to old men!"

"Yes, but the boys will *die* if you don't remove your curse!" Izzy cried.

While the goddess was distracted, Rosie inched towards her, clutching Cupid's arrow behind her back.

"I'm afraid there is no turning back," Juventas said coldly. "And if you don't speak to me with a little more respect, then I'll turn *you* into a baby!"

Rosie realized that she had better act quickly, before Izzy ended up cursed as well! Stealthily she reached out towards Juventas, and grazed the goddess's hand with the tip of Cupid's golden arrow.

The goddess yelped in surprise, and turned towards Rosie in fury. "How *dare* you attack me, mortal!" she demanded, advancing on Rosie and raising her hands. Blue sparks flickered at her fingertips.

Oh, no! Rosie thought in terror. The arrow hasn't worked. Now, she's going to cast a spell on me!

Chapter Ten

A ball of blue fire formed in Juventas's hands, and she was about to hurl it at Rosie when a change seemed to come over her. The goddess shook her head, confused, and the ball of fire fizzled away. As she looked up, her gaze fell on Rosie, and Juventas gave her a dazzling smile.

"Hello, who are you?" the goddess asked sweetly.

"Hello," Rosie said. "I'm Rosie, and this is Princess Isidora."

"Why, what pretty girls!" Juventas said, smiling. "And with such charming manners. What brings you here, my dears?"

"We came to beg you to remove your curse on the boys of Rome," Izzy explained, dropping into a deep curtsey.

"Curse?" the goddess asked, frowning as if she was trying to remember something that seemed very far away. At last she nodded. "Oh, that," she said vaguely. "Yes, of course I'll remove it. I can't think why I didn't do so before. Those poor boys have been punished enough." She waved a hand, and blue sparks crackled around her fingertips again. Then she beamed at the girls. "It is done," she said. "The boys are all boys once more."

Izzy threw her arms around Juventas. "Thank you!" she cried in delight.

The goddess looked a little surprised, but patted Izzy's head kindly. "You are most welcome, dear," she told her.

Suddenly the peace of the garden was shattered by a terrible roaring noise. Rosie

whipped round anxiously, wondering if the
Harpies had somehow forced their way into
the Garden of Heaven. But instead she saw
a very angry Mercury marching towards
her, followed by a tired-looking Cupid.
Rosie glanced down guiltily at her feet –
she and Izzy were still wearing Mercury's
winged sandals!

Mercury pointed at the girls. "Give me
those sandals back!" he ordered, his cheeks
purple with rage. "Without them, I can't get
anywhere! Cupid had to fly me all the way
here, you know."

Rosie and Izzy slipped off the sandals at

once, and handed them to Mercury. "We're very sorry," Rosie said.

"Yes, we were going to bring them right back, honestly," Izzy added.

Juventas put a consoling arm around Mercury. "They came here for a good reason, Mercury," she said. "Do not be too hard on them."

Cupid's eyes lit up when he heard the soft tone of Juventas's voice. He grinned at the girls. "You did it, didn't you?" he asked. "You used my arrow!"

Rosie grinned at him. "Yes, and Juventas has removed her curse! The boys aren't old men any more."

Cupid whooped with joy, and was just about to zoom off happily when he stopped and turned back. "You know," he said thoughtfully, "you two aren't so bad – for *girls*!"

Rosie grinned at him, and gave him back his arrow. "Careful," she warned teasingly. "Anyone would think you were God of Love or something!"

Cupid zipped away happily and Rosie turned back to Izzy. "There's just one problem," she said to her friend. "How are we going to get back to earth without the magic sandals?"

Izzy bit her lip nervously. "Oh, I hadn't thought of that," she said, looking worried.

Juventas must have overheard their conversation, for she immediately came over to the girls. "Don't worry, you two. I'll send you back to Rome on a magic cloud," she told them kindly.

"That would be wonderful," Izzy said, "but, you see, there are some Harpies after us, and so it might not be safe."

Juventas waved a hand airily. "Don't worry about them," she said. "Pluto will have summoned them back to the Underworld now. He knows his cause is lost. And, besides, they wouldn't dare touch you while you are under my protection." She clapped her hands commandingly, and a fluffy white cloud in

the shape of a swan appeared. It hovered in
front of the girls. "Climb on," Juventas said.
"It's quite safe, I promise."

Rosie and Izzy stepped carefully onto the
swan-shaped cloud. It was like stepping onto
cotton wool, Rosie thought, her feet sinking
into the fluffy whiteness.

"Thank you so much," she said, smiling at
Juventas. "Goodbye!"

"Goodbye, Mercury!" Izzy added happily as the cloud began to drift away. "We're off!"

The girls sat tight as the cloud carried them gently back to the palace gardens, and then melted away.

At that very moment, a young man came running round the corner of the palace and stopped when he saw the girls.

"Marcus!" Izzy cried, running over and hugging him. "You're sixteen again!"

"I know," Marcus grinned, hugging her back. "Isn't it great?" He pointed up at the sky. "I was just looking for you, Izzy," he went on. "I saw the most amazing cloud up there – it looked exactly like a swan!"

Izzy smiled at Rosie knowingly. "It sounds beautiful," she said.

"It was," Marcus replied. "Anyway, I'd better run. I'm going to find all my friends and see if they're back to normal too. I've really missed them!"

As Marcus raced off across the lawn, Izzy turned to Rosie. "Thank you, Rosie," she said. "I couldn't have saved Marcus without you."

"It was a pleasure," Rosie said, and then she laughed. "Well, apart from being chased by Harpies, of course!" she added. She looked around the gardens, trying to drink in every detail. She never wanted to forget this adventure. "I think I'd better go home now, Izzy," she said reluctantly.

"Will you come back another day?" Izzy asked hopefully.

Rosie smiled. "I certainly will," she said, hugging her new friend. "Goodbye, Izzy."

As soon as she had said farewell, a whirlwind whipped up around her. She just heard Izzy say, "Goodbye, Rosie," before the Roman palace became a blur, and Rosie felt herself spinning through the air.

In no time at all, her feet touched solid ground and she opened her eyes. She was back in front of the mosaic, in her great-aunt's castle.

But Rosie saw that the picture had changed! Now the princess was smiling and sitting on the lawn with her brother, pointing up at the clouds in the sky. Rosie smiled at the happy scene – and then her eye was caught by a tiny detail in the top corner that she hadn't noticed before. A tiny winged Cupid was flying through the sky, with a golden bow and arrow.

"Rosie! Hey, Rosie!" came a voice from
behind her, and Rosie turned to see Luke
racing down the passageway towards her,
clutching a piece of paper. "Will you test me
on my spellings?" he asked. "Because I've just
got to beat Anna tomorrow. I couldn't bear it
if I was beaten by a girl."

Rosie laughed. "OK," she said. "But let's go back to the kitchen, where it's warmer."

Luke passed her the paper, and they set off together along the corridor.

As they walked, Rosie looked at the first word and smiled. "So, Luke, how do you spell CLOUD?" she asked.

THE END

Did you enjoy reading about Rosie's
adventure with the Cloud Princess?
If you did, you'll love the next
Little Princesses
book!

Turn over to read the first chapter of
The Sea Princess.

Chapter One

"Rosie, what are you doing?"

Rosie Campbell looked up from where she was lying on her bed to see her little brother Luke in the doorway. "I'm reading this," she said, holding up the joke book she'd been looking at. "Emily lent it to me at school today. Why?"

"I've got a question," Luke said. He ran in and leaped onto Rosie's bed beside her. "It's for my school project on sea creatures."

Rosie put her book down and sat up. "Go on, then," she said.

"Well," Luke began, "today, we learned about octopuses. Did you know that they squirt out black ink when they're scared?"

Rosie shook her head.

"And yesterday we learned about dolphins," Luke went on. "Mrs Lovell told us that when they're asleep, one side of their brain is still awake!"

"Cool!" Rosie replied.

"But what I really want to know is, where do all the mermaids live?" Luke asked eagerly.

Rosie smiled. "Sorry, Luke," she said. "Mermaids don't really exist. They're just in stories."

Luke shook his head stubbornly. "No,

they're real," he said. "Great-aunt Rosamund said so."

Luke had an obstinate look on his face. "When she came to visit us last year, she told me that she had met a mermaid before," he told Rosie. "And she said that the mermaid looked just like the one on the fountain in her garden."

Rosie stared at her brother with interest. "She really said that?" Rosie asked. "That she met a mermaid?"

"Yes!" Luke said. "And—"

But before he could say anything else, a shout floated up from downstairs. "Luke! Are you up there? Tom's on the phone for you!" called Mr Campbell.

Luke's eyes brightened. Tom was his best friend from home. "Coming, Dad!" he shouted, racing out of Rosie's bedroom at once.

"Wait!" Rosie called, but Luke had already gone. Rosie jumped off her bed, feeling a prickle of excitement. She knew that Great-aunt Rosamund might well have made up the mermaid story to entertain Luke, but she couldn't help hoping that there might be some truth in it. Great-aunt Rosamund had certainly met all sorts of other extraordinary people – as Rosie had been finding out for herself!

Rosie rushed out of her bedroom and down the spiral staircase. She was dying to go and see the mermaid fountain now. She had never really paid it much attention before. Great-aunt Rosamund's castle was full of the most fabulous treasures, and Rosie was always discovering new things.

Rosie grinned as she threw on her coat and raced out of the back door and across the grass. She knew that at the end of this particular stretch of lawn, there was a lavender garden with a small stone fountain at its centre.

Rosie ran through the lavender bushes until she reached the fountain. She looked at it carefully. It had once been white, but it was now weathered to grey. The bowl of the fountain had sloping sides and was carved all over with images of mermaids and mermen, dolphins and fish. Right in the middle of the fountain, rising out of the bowl, was a statue of a young mermaid sitting on a rock.

Rosie felt her heart leap as she noticed the stone crown on top of the mermaid statue's long hair. If she's wearing a crown, surely she must be another little princess! Rosie thought excitedly.

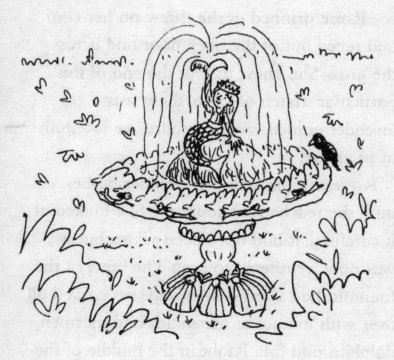

Eagerly, she bobbed a curtsey and said a breathless, "Hello!" to the little mermaid.

Instantly, a gust of wind picked up from nowhere and whirled around Rosie, lifting her off her feet. Rosie could smell the salty tang of sea air, and hear the beautiful, haunting sound of singing. Another adventure was beginning . . .

Read the rest of *The Sea Princess* to find out what happens next!

Little Princesses
The Golden Princess

Katie Chase

Rosie knows a very special secret.
Hidden in her great-aunt's mysterious
Scottish castle are lots of little princesses for
her to find. And each one will whisk
her away to another part of the
world on a magical adventure!

Chayna, the Golden Princess, is sure that
the High Priest is tricking her people into
thinking that the Sun God is angry with
them. The answer lies deep inside the
temple in the City of Gold, but Rosie and
Chayna must avoid the traps in order to reach it!

Join Rosie and meet her exciting new friends,
as she discovers all the Little Princesses.

978 0 099 48843 9